Four Hens
and a
Rooster

Rabén & Sjögren Bokförlag, Stockholm
www.raben.se
Translation copyright © 2005 by Rabén & Sjögren Bokförlag
Originally published in Sweden by Rabén & Sjögren under the title *Fyra hönor och en tupp*
Text copyright © 2004 by Lena Landström
Pictures copyright © 2004 by Olof Landström
All rights reserved
Distributed in Canada by Douglas & McIntyre Publishing Group
Library of Congress Control Number: 2004097390
Printed in Denmark
First American edition, 2005
ISBN-13: 978-91-29-66336-5
ISBN-10: 91-29-66336-9

Rabén & Sjögren Bokförlag is part of
P. A. Norstedt & Söner Publishing Group, established in 1823

Lena Landström
Pictures by Olof Landström

Four Hens
and a
Rooster

Translated by Joan Sandin

R&S
BOOKS

Stockholm   New York   London   Adelaide   Toronto

There once was a chicken yard with four hens: a brown hen, a beige hen, a blond hen, and a red hen.

A little rooster lived there, too.

"What a nice little rooster you have here," said everyone who came to visit.
"Yes, indeed," said the hens.
The rooster paid no attention whatsoever to the hens. He was much too busy with his own important project. The hens were welcome to be in his chicken yard, as long as they didn't disturb him with their clucking.

Every day, food was served in a long trough.
Each one had a place at the trough to peck away at the delicious kernels of corn, freshly cooked potato skins, grated carrots, and juicy little dandelion leaves.

Above each place was a sign with a name.
The first one said "Brown," the second "Beige," the third "Blond," and the

fourth "Red." The fifth one said "Rooster."

But the hens wondered why the rooster's place was so big and their places were so small. They clucked softly to one another so they wouldn't disturb the rooster. Had the rooster ever thought about how big his place was and how small theirs were? They wondered if the rooster would be offended if they asked him about it.

One day, when portions had been on the stingy side, the four hens decided to take a chance and ask him. Carefully, they approached the rooster, who was bent over his drawing.
"Ahem! We were wondering if maybe we could . . ." began the brown hen cautiously.
"We were thinking . . ."

"Hens shouldn't think!" crowed the rooster. "*I'm* the one who thinks around here!" he declared, his voice cracking.

The hens had never seen the rooster so angry. The beige hen passed out. "But we think our places at the feeding trough are so small," said the brown hen.

With that, the rooster stomped off.

He soon returned with two booster roosters from the neighboring farm, one on each side.

All pumped-up and serious, the three roosters stepped up close to the brown hen and crowed so loud that she almost lost her hearing.
The other hens threw themselves to the ground and said, "We don't think anything! We'll do exactly what you want—if that's what you want."

The little rooster thought that sounded fine. Stepping high, he went back to his own business. And the two booster roosters went back home.

The hens started having strange dreams at night.

Finally, the blond hen, who was the oldest, said, "We can't go on like this. We must do something. We'll take a course in self-esteem."

The hens were feeling dizzy when they got off the bus.
The instructor passed out Power Bars and sport drinks.

The hens learned all they needed to know in their class:

Strength training.

Relaxation.

Feather fluffing
and concentration.

Deep breathing and
voice training.

And they worked together in small groups.

When the hens got home, the rooster was making some new signs.
"Deep breathing," whispered Beige. And all four breathed deeply from
the stomach.
"Feather fluffing!" whispered Blond. And all four fluffed up their feathers.
"Concentration," whispered Red.

And then, together in their deep new voices, all four hens said:

"We—want—our—fair—share."

The rooster knocked over his can of paint. "But . . ." he said.
"No buts," said the hens.

Then Red and Blond took down all the signs. Brown got a long measuring
tape and Beige borrowed the rooster's calculator. They measured the
feeding trough and divided it into five equal places: one for Brown, one for
Beige, one for Blond, one for Red. And one for the rooster.

What a nuisance, thought the rooster, hanging his head.
What should he do now?
And what was that over there? His important project!
He had completely forgotten about it!

The sun was shining in the chicken yard. The hens were clucking in their beautiful new voices. And the rooster was working on his project. New problems had turned up that needed to be solved.

"What a nice, contented rooster you have here," said two hens who had come to visit.

"Yes, indeed," answered Brown, Beige, Blond, and Red.

And then they invited the guests to help themselves to all the delicious kernels of corn, freshly cooked potato skins, grated carrots, and juicy little dandelion leaves that their hearts desired.